Be sure to look for all the great McGee and Me! books and videos at your favorite bookstore.

Focus on the Family

PRESENTS

THE NEW ADVENTURES

McGEE and me!

Beauty in the Least

Bill Myers and Robert E. West

Based upon characters created by Bill Myers and Ken E. Johnson, the story by George Taweel and Rob Loos, and the teleplay by David N. Weiss and Rob McFarlane.

Tyndale House Publishers, Inc.
Wheaton, Illinois

For Grandma . . . with love, appreciation, and fondest of memories.

Library of Congress Cataloging-in-Publication Data

Myers, Bill, date
      Beauty in the least / Bill Myers and Robert E. West.
         p.   cm.
      "Focus on the family presents McGee and me!"
      "12"—Spine.
      "Based upon characters created by Bill Myers and Ken E. Johnson,
the story by George Taweel and Rob Loos, and the teleplay by David
N. Weiss and Rob McFarlane."
      Summary: Nick and his cartoon creation, McGee, get a crash course
in friendship—and a lesson about homelessness—when Nick's Romanian
penpal and his father show up for an unexpected visit.
      ISBN 0-8423-4124-2 (SC) :
      [1. Friendship—Fiction.   2. Homeless persons—Fiction.
3. Cartoon characters—Fiction.   4. Christian life—Fiction.]
I. West, Robert, date   .   II. Title.
PZ7.M98234Be   1993
[Fic]—dc20   93-14026

Contents

"You must love your neighbor just as much as you love yourself." (Matthew 22:39, *The Living Bible*)

ONE
Things That Go Bump in the Night

"Mc-Gee, Mc-Gee, Mc-Gee . . ."

The crowd continued to chant, demanding that I, the All-American everything, once again step onto the playing field. There were just seconds left in Slobber Bowl XXXXXXXXXXXXXVII and, as usual, the day could only be saved by the magnificent and marvelously macho . . . McGee.

My team, the Anaheim Arm Pits (imagine how hard it was to find a mascot), was down by two points. One precise punt by me, their perfectly punctual punter, would clinch the championship. But after running twenty or thirty touchdowns (almost half in the right direction), kicking 23.5 field goals, and eating twice my weight in (burp) corn dogs, this poised and professionally polished punter was plainly too pooped (and plump) to punt.

"Mc-Gee, Mc-Gee, Mc-Gee . . ."

But what about my team?

What about my fans?

What about all that money I'd make selling sports shoes on TV?

Say no more. I waddled onto the field as only a wide-bodied eating machine can waddle. (Don't worry, I can shed these pounds with just a few quick strokes of an eraser. Being a pencil drawing does have a few advantages . . . just keep me away from those paper shredders). But I digress. Or is it digest. Hmmm, that makes me hungry— think I'll grab another corn dog for the road.

Where were we? Oh yes. I stepped onto the field. Suddenly the stadium was filled with the roar of fans, the flash of photographers, and the face of a giant outer-space monster.

A WHAT??

You guessed her, Chester. As usual, being a sports superstar was not enough for someone with my enormous ego. Now I was also being called upon to save the Earth from another invasion of outer-space giants.

I watched as the ugly creature leaned forward and stuck his giant snout down on the playing field.

Fans fled. Referees ran. Quarterbacks quaked.

But not me. No-siree-bob. I'm the hero of this story. A legend in my own mind.

The giant monster opened his giant mouth and with all of his giant fury roared, "McGEE!!!"

Suddenly the cheering fans disappeared. More suddenly still, the playing field turned into a kitchen table. Most suddenliest stiller, I was no longer holding a football, but an eraser.

Yes, once again, Nicholas Martin, my part-time

creator and full-time killjoy was interrupting another one of my fabulous fantasies.

"Have you seen my eraser?" he asked as he shoved books and papers around the kitchen table.

Poor kid. As usual he was coming to me for help. And as usual I had the solution. "This what you mean, Nickster?" I quipped as I twirled the ex-football now-eraser on my finger.

"Yeah," he sighed, "I need that for this history report."

Luckily I had other ideas. "C'mon, kid, loosen up," I shouted as I tucked the eraser under my arm. "Let's make a little history of our own. A sports moment. You know . . . the thrill of victory, the agony of . . . er, well, forget that part."

Before he could argue, my marvelous imagination went into overdrive. The kitchen table became a stadium as I began to run a zigzag pattern, straight-arming everything in sight—the pencil holder, Nick's glass of milk, Mom's flower arrangement.

"He's to the thirty . . . the forty . . . midfield!" I cried doing my own play by play. "It's the run of the decade! Twelve broken tackles, five perfect reverses, and a partridge in a pear tree."

"Oh, brother," Nick groaned.

Then it happened. I got broadsided by Nick's popcorn bowl. It was a hard tackle and a lousy break, but I wasn't worried. That just meant it was time for another preeminent punt. Once again the crowd chanted my name:

"Mc-GEE, Mc-GEE, Mc-GEE . . ."

(What'd you expect them to chant? "Bugs

Bunny?" "Mickey Mouse?" No way! Let those jokers find their own book series.)

Everyone waited as I prepared to punt the Pink Pearl (uh, you know, that's a brand of eraser . . . aw, never mind) to Pluto.

"But can the mighty McGee do it?" the announcer cried. "Although he is loved by every created creature . . . although he is the embodiment of everything great, noble, and, of course, humble, can he—"

"OK, McGee," Nick interrupted again. You could tell his patience was about gone. "I've got to finish this history report, so hand me the eraser."

"But there's only three seconds left," I protested. "We're two points behind. What about my team, my fans . . . what about the readers of this book? They've just waded through three pages of this football fantasy, and if there's no payoff they're really going to be ticked."

But the look on Nicky boy's face said he didn't give a rip about you . . . or me. So I quickly raced forward and kicked that eraser-ball for all I was worth (which, with the cost of paper and colored felt pens, is about $1.82).

"It's up!" I shouted. "It has the distance! It's . . . It's . . . caught by the idiot giant boy!"

Sure enough, ol' Nick caught the football and calmly went back to erasing with it.

My field became a kitchen table, and once again we were back to reality with all its boringness.

"Look," Nick sighed, "I know you're excited about our visiting Louis in Indianapolis this weekend. After all, it's our first time to see a professional football team, but if I don't get this report written we may as well kiss those fifty-yard-line seats good-bye."

Nick pulled his paper forward and continued erasing.

"OK, keep working, Einstein," I muttered. "But how 'bout one last pass for old time's sake."

"McGee . . ."

"Please . . ."

"McGee . . ."

I could tell he was weakening. So, not having an ounce of pride in my humble body, I did what any quivering pile of pridelessness would do. I begged.

"Please-please-please-please-please-please-please . . ."

"All right . . . all right!" Nick cried.

That's all it took. In a flash I was racing across the table.

"McGee's going long!" I shouted. "He's deep! Martin's going to throw the bomb!!!"

Nick fired the eraser.

It sailed towards me.

I leaped into the air.

I caught the ball.

I looked down.

I suddenly wondered why they didn't make kitchen tables as long as they used to.

I smiled sadly to Nick. Then waved. Then dropped out of sight faster than Wile E. Coyote in a Roadrunner cartoon.

"Whooooooaaaaaa!!!"

CRASH-BOOM-TINKLE-TINKLE.

The "Whooooooaaaaaa!!!" was me.

The "CRASH-BOOM" was my body hitting the floor.

And the "TINKLE-TINKLE?"

Got me. Though I noticed I did seem to be missing quite a few teeth.

Nick shook his head at McGee, then picked up his pencil and went back to writing. He stopped only long enough to glance at his notes and check the information in the books he had opened.

No doubt about it, Nicholas wanted to go to that Colts-Bills game with Louis. Wanted it bad. Real bad. So bad that he was willing to do just about anything . . . even ruin his reputation as a hater of history by getting a decent grade on his history report. That was the condition his folks made in order for him to go. Nothing like a little parental blackmail to improve the ol' GPA.

This meant Nick had been busy. So busy that he didn't even play his standard $8\frac{1}{2}$ hours of Game Boy that night. So busy that he stayed up after the rest of the family went to bed. So busy that he didn't notice a shadow as it slowly passed across the dining room window.

A SHADOW??

Hang on, there's more.

Nicholas flipped through the pages of another book, jotting down more information. Finally he'd had enough. Pro game or no pro game, he could barely keep his eyes open. It was definitely time to hit the hay. He slammed the book shut. He looked up. And—

He froze!

14

There it was. A shadow. Only now it was on the far wall, looming several times larger than life. After a couple of seconds of raw fear, Nick forced himself to move. Slowly he turned to look out the window and saw . . .

Nothing.

He glanced back to the wall again.

More of nothing. The shadow was gone.

He blinked, then frowned. What was going on? Nick wasn't sure, but he knew he better find out. Quietly, he slipped from the dining room chair and crept up to the side of the window. He took a deep breath. Then, with a rush of courage, he leaped in front of the glass to face the monster head-on!

But all he faced was even more of nothing.

This was getting too weird. Nick gulped. As far as he was concerned he'd put in enough time as a superhero for one evening. Now if he could just get to the stairs, race up to his room, and dive under the covers of his bed, he'd call it a day.

The only problem was that the stairs were all the way on the other side of the room. Then there was another little matter: the knob to the back door had suddenly started to rattle!

Someone was trying to get in!!

Well, it was now or never. If Nick was going to prove he was a coward he'd have to hurry and do it, before he got killed! With a spurt of speed he raced across the room, took the steps three at a time, darted into the upstairs hallway, and ran smack dab into . . .

"AUGHHHH!" Dad cried.

"AUGHHHH!" Nick answered.

They hit the ground at roughly the same time.

"What are you doing up?" Nicholas asked as he scrambled back to his feet. Then he pointed to the seven iron in Dad's hands. "And why are you carrying that golf club?"

"I thought I heard somebody in the backyard," Dad answered.

"Not anymore," Nick said. "Now they're at the back door!"

Dad winced. "Well, I guess it's up to us to save your mother and sisters," he said.

"Why couldn't I have had brothers?" Nick groaned.

Dad gave him a look. "Come on, follow me."

Reluctantly Nick obeyed as they started back toward the stairs. Carefully, step-by-step, they inched their way down.

"He was right outside," Nicholas whispered.

Dad nodded.

Once they reached the bottom of the stairs Dad snapped off the lights. "Stay here," he whispered. "I'll go check."

Nick was more than happy to obey as his father quietly crept toward the windows.

Dad checked the first window.

Nothing.

Then the second.

Nothing again.

The third.

More nothing.

Finally he arrived at the back door. Carefully he reached for the lock and unbolted it. After a deep breath he slowly turned the nob. Then, raising his club in preparation, he quickly threw open the door to see . . .

You guessed it: even more of nothing.

He let out a low sigh of relief. "Well, whoever it was is gone now," Dad said as he lowered his golf club. He walked back to the staircase and casually flipped on the light only to be met by:

"AUGH!"

"AUGHHHHH!"

"AUGHHHHHHHHHH!"

The little chorus of screams was brought to you by:

Mom holding a radio telephone . . .

Grandma toting a yardstick . . .

And Sarah wearing enough green mud on her face to scare away any burglar.

Dad broke out laughing as he surveyed all three women poised at the bottom of the stairs, ready to defend their home. "I pity anyone who tries to break into this house," he said. "But have no fear, ladies, the men are—"

A loud bang at the door made Dad finish his sentence with a yelp: *"Here!"*

In keeping with family tradition, everyone panicked. Dad dropped his seven iron and tripped over Nick, who had dropped to the floor. Mom dropped the portable phone and kept colliding with Grandma, who wrung her hands and paced in little circles.

Luckily, Sarah was safe and sound—under the kitchen table.

"What's the phone number for 911?" Mom kept crying.

Dad and Nick were too busy stumbling over each other and the golf club to answer. Finally Dad freed his club from Nick's feet just as the silhouetted figure reappeared in the window. Immediately it began banging on the glass and shouting incoherently.

"Look, Dad!" Nicholas said, pointing. "He's holding a sign or something."

Dad rushed to the door and turned on the porch light. Suddenly the silhouette became a man. A man nearly Dad's age. The paper he held to the glass was an airline ticket folder with the name "Romanian Air."

Below this was a handwritten note. With his seven iron raised to strike, Dad moved closer. He tried to read the note, but his glasses were up in his room. Grandma's knitting basket was nearby so he reached into it and pulled out her glasses—complete with glittering jewels and rhinestone rims. He tilted them back and forth until he was finally able to focus them on the note.

"'Michael and Ilie,'" he read. "From Romania."

"Ilie?!" Nick cried as he rushed toward the door.

"Who?" Dad asked.

The figure outside suddenly hoisted up a small boy and held him in the window for all to see, as Nick jerked open the door.

"It's Ilie Tinescu," he cried. "My pen pal from Romania!"

TWO
Untimely Visitors

Nick turned from the window where the visitors stood and shrugged sheepishly to his family. To say he was embarrassed might be an understatement. To say his face was glowing like the inside of a toaster oven would be more accurate.

"Well," Dad said, returning Grandma's glasses to her basket, "I guess we should ask them in."

"I can't meet anyone looking like this!" Sarah cried, pointing to the green mud on her face. Quickly she turned and dashed back up the stairs.

Dad straightened his pajamas and walked to the open door. He was about to apologize to the guy standing there when the man's two burly arms suddenly caught him up in the world's biggest bear hug.

"Dom mnu lay, Martoni!" the huge man cried in Romanian. At least everybody guessed it was Romanian.

Dad wheezed and tried to catch his breath. Then, just about the time he was wondering if he'd have to see a chiropractor for the rest of his life, the big guy let go.

"I am Michael Tinescu," the man said in accented English, "and this is my son, Ilie."

"Hello, Meester Martin," Ilie said to Nick. "I can't believe I finally meet you after four years!" Although the boy had his dad's broad smile, he definitely didn't have his size. In fact he was at least a foot shorter than Nick, something the pictures they'd traded hadn't shown.

"Ilie, is it really you?" Nick asked, staring at him. "You're so . . . small."

"And you are so . . . beeg!" Ilie returned cheerfully. Then, very politely, he turned to each of the other family members: "Hello, Meester Martin. Hello, Meesus Martin. Hello . . . uh . . . Grandma. Ees not correct?" he asked hesitantly.

"Very correct," Grandma answered in her usual gracious manner. "Nice to meet you, Ilie."

Ilie looked around questioningly. "But vere ees Jamie . . . and Sarah?"

"Hi, I'm Sarah." All eyes turned to see Sarah bounding down the stairs. In one brief minute she had gone from a green-faced monster to an elegantly dressed teen. "I was just looking in on Jamie," she lied. "She has a pretty bad case of the measles."

Nice save, Nick thought.

"Ahhhhh, *pooh-zah,*" Ilie exclaimed. He gestured to imaginary spots on his face. "I already had *pooh-zah . . .* uh . . . measles, as you say."

"Mom's got Jamie quarantined up in her room," Sarah added. She looked down at Ilie then glanced

20

over at Nick as if to say, *Isn't he a little small to be your pen pal?*

Nick just gave her a look back that said, *Why don't you go back to your swamp!*

(Isn't brother-sister communication amazing?)

"Sarah," Michael interrupted with great emotion. "Caring for your seester when she has the measles . . . true American kindness."

Sarah nodded in embarrassment. She wasn't crazy about lying, but how do you tell a foreigner that you were wearing green mud all over your face? And how do you explain that if you had greeted them in it, they'd have been halfway back across the Atlantic by now . . . without a boat?

"Ah, excuse the way the rest of us are dressed," Mom spoke up. She pulled her robe about her and stepped up to Michael. "But Nick wasn't expecting Ilie until Lent, so—"

"Lent? *Ja,* of course, ve're right on time," Michael said, shaking her hand. "Today ees first day of our Christmas Lenten season. The relief organization I vork for send me and Ilie to USA, to big meeting in Meessh-ee-gun."

Michael's English wasn't the best, and it took a little effort to figure out what he said as he continued. "But if we are inquisition . . . " (chances are he meant "imposition"). He turned and motioned his son toward the door. "Come, Ilie, upon these nice people we must not untrude." (Chances are he meant "intrude.")

Either way you say it, the Martins realized a major mistake had been made about the dates of

Ilie's visit, and now the two Romanians were about to leave.

Nick hurried forward. "No, no, you aren't . . . 'untruding.'" He turned to his mother. "Are they, Mom?"

Of course, they'd all been expecting Ilie's visit. Sure, they'd thought it was happening in about another six months, but it wasn't Michael and Ilie's fault that Romanians celebrate Lent at a different time of year than Americans.

"Why, no. Of course not," Mom exclaimed, trying to sound sincere. "Please stay," she insisted. Suddenly she noticed Dad still clutching his golf club. "Ahhhh, David," she murmured, giving him an elbow.

Dad looked down and saw the club in his hand. He quickly grinned. "Oh! . . . ah . . . just practicing," he said, giving the club a few twists of the wrist. Then he awkwardly set it aside and asked, "Can we help you with your bags?"

"No, ve have only zees one," Michael answered.

"Only one bag?" Mom asked.

"Romania, she ess not a rich country," Michael explained. "Much vee do not have."

"Oh," Dad said a little embarrassed. "Well, listen, come on and follow me upstairs. Sarah, you can move in with Grandma for the night. And Nick, if you'll get the cot from the basement, Ilie can stay in your room."

Ilie whooped out something in Romanian.

"Uh . . . right. Sure," Nick answered, not having a clue what the boy had said.

As Dad led Michael and Ilie up the stairs, Mom called to them, "Can I get you anything to eat?"

"No thank you, Meesus Martin," Michael called back down. "Ve have late dinner."

Just before they disappeared, Michael turned to his son and spoke in Romanian again, *"Iubeste vecinul t'au."*

Nick stood near the kitchen table and gave a shrug. Once again he hadn't a clue about what was just said.

Fortunately ol' Nicky boy had left my sketchpad on the table, so I'd heard the whole thing. Yeah, it's me, the marvelous McGee again, and all I had to say was . . .

Romanians, my foot.

"Hey, Nick," I whispered. "Did you hear that secret code! They look like Soviet agents to me."

Nick rolled his eyes. "They were speaking Romanian, McGee. Besides, there are no more Soviet agents," he whispered, glancing up toward the staircase.

"Don't tell me you buy that whole collapse of the Soviet Union thing," I scorned. "Pure propaganda."

Suddenly there was a loud buzzer. Obviously the timing device to some bomb that was about to go off. So being the world-renowned and courageous secret agent I am, I did what any world-renowned and courageous secret agent would do . . . I leaped back into the sketchpad and hid for my life.

Nick did a little leaping too . . . until he noticed the buzzing came from an intercom he had rigged up for Jamie on the kitchen counter. He sighed and shook his head. After tonight he wondered if his nerves were ever going to be the same.

"This is Jamie," a voice said from the speaker. "Can you bring me some ginger ale? . . . and a graham cracker?"

Nick groaned and crossed over to the contraption. He pushed the button above the speaker. "Plain or cinnamon?" he asked.

"Ahhhhh . . . one of each," the voice answered.

Nick headed for the cupboard wondering if making the intercom for his sick sister had been such a good idea after all.

A few minutes later Nicholas was in his bedroom arm wrestling with an old army cot. The legs were going every which way except down.

Meanwhile, Ilie was taking in the sights of Nick's room like it was Disneyland. "Eet ees just as I imagined from your letters! You are so lucky to live een such a place."

Suddenly he noticed Nick's computer screen. On it was a sketch of McGee. "Ahhh, a computer with your McGee drawing!" He crossed to it, staring wide-eyed. "Amazink!"

"Yeah, that's kinda new," Nick said as he continued to fight the legs of the cot.

"Eet ees so amazink," Ilie went on as he reached out to touch a button on the side. "Vat do zese button do?"

He soon had his answer. The screen completely blanked out. He had turned off the computer.

Nick looked up, his face draining of color.

24

"Ahhhhh . . . no problem," he said with a gulp. "I just wish I'd saved it first."

Continuing his tour of the room, Ilie noticed a bright red model glider bracketed to the wall above Nick's bed. "Zees ees vonderful, Nick. . . . Zees must be ze model plane you wrote about!" He took his shoes off and stood on the bed, shifting the glider about for a better look.

Suddenly very protective of his things, Nick tried the old distraction routine. "Uhhh . . . did you ever finish the model you wrote about—you know, that ship with the Romanian name?"

"The *Carpaithia?*" Ilie asked, turning away from the glider. "I finished eet, but I no longer have eet," he said as he stepped off the bed. "I needed ze wood for anozer project, so . . . "

As Ilie talked, Nick edged over to the bed and readjusted the glider. It wouldn't do for things to get out of kilter just because somebody dropped in for a visit.

Next, Ilie noticed Nicholas's Game Boy. Nick immediately stiffened with fear as the kid picked it up. He wanted to yank it out of Ilie's hands, but somehow he figured that wouldn't exactly help international relations.

Luckily, Ilie was suddenly distracted by Nick's skateboard. Before Nick had time to protest, Ilie had hopped on it and started zipping across the room toward the art table. "I see zees in movie— *Back to zee Future,*" he exclaimed.

Unfortunately, nobody in the movie had said anything about how to stop! Nick dove for him and swung him off just as the board sailed under the table.

"Uh . . . thanks, Neeck," Ilie said with a nervous laugh. "I could use a leetle practice, maybe in a much beeger place."

"Right," Nick nodded. His nerves on edge, he returned to fixing the impossible-to-fix cot. "Hey," he said, trying to change the subject, "what was that your dad said to you in Romanian just before you came up the stairs?"

Ilie reached into his duffel bag and pulled out a Romanian Bible. "Eet ees from Matthew twenty-two," he said as he thumbed through the pages. "You must know zees one, Nick. *Iubeste vecinul t'au iubeste vencinu.'*"

"Uh . . . ," Nick hedged, "mine must be a different translation."

"Ah," Ilie laughed, "een English eet means you must love your neighbor just as much as you love yourself."

"Oh, sure," Nicholas agreed. "I know that one."

Ilie nodded in satisfaction and turned back to rummage in his duffel bag. Nick craned his neck for a better look. He wondered what foreign and exotic things Ilie had stashed inside. Finally with great flourish the boy pulled out—

"A toothbrush?" Nicholas asked in surprise.

"Yes." Ilie agreed with a grin. "My very own. Now, could you tell me vhere ees zee . . . zee—" He couldn't seem to find the word.

"The bathroom?" Nick volunteered.

"Yes . . . yes . . . zee bassroom," Ilie repeated.

"Down the hall," Nick said, trying not to laugh. "First door on the right."

Ilie closed his bag and started for the door. Then he turned with an even bigger grin. "I can't believe vee get to stay here a whole veek!" With that he headed back down the hall.

Nick stared after him. "A week!" he gasped. What about Louis? What about the Colts-Bills game?! He couldn't just leave Ilie here while he took off for Indianapolis. Could he?

Suddenly things weren't turning out so well. In fact, they were turning out pretty awful. Sure, Nick had been excited about meeting Ilie . . . but talk about lousy timing!

In disgust he plopped down on the cot, which immediately collapsed under his weight.

THREE
Busy Bodies

RIIIING!

Mom ignored the doorbell and continued working in the kitchen.

RIIIING!

More ignoring. More working.

RIIIING!

Even more ignoring. Even more . . . well, you probably get the picture. The reason was simple. The doorbell had been ringing all morning. And by "all morning" we're not just talking all morning; we're talking *ALL MORNING.*

You see, Michael had volunteered to fix it. And fixing it meant ringing it. Unfortunately, the ringing bell was on the kitchen wall right above where Mom was working . . . which probably explains why she was getting "rung out."

"I've got to make something for their dinner," she muttered while thumbing through a cookbook. "Ahh, what's this . . . 'Romanian Cabbage Casserole' . . . " She read on, "Hollow a large summer squash. Add six heads of green cabbage and steam 'til limp."

RIIIING!

Mom jumped for the hundredth time. But this was a "new and improved" jump. This time she dropped the book, which hit the rolling pin, which crashed into a tomato, which rolled off the counter nearly becoming pizza sauce . . . until Mom made one of her famous catches.

"That doorbell is driving me nuts!" she cried.

Now, as we all know, Mom's pretty cool under pressure. But with Thanksgiving coming up, instant house guests, a little girl with measles, and nonstop ringing bells . . . well, she was definitely showing signs of thermonuclear meltdown.

Then, just as Michael walked in, Jamie's intercom suddenly buzzed. "Not to vorry," Michael said cheerfully, "I am almost finished." He began adjusting the bell above her.

"Just a minute, honey," Mom called into the intercom.

Michael looked at her nervously. He'd heard of American friendliness, but calling near strangers "honey" seemed a bit much. Before the woman could hit him with a "sweetheart" or a "darling," he changed the subject.

"Back home," he said, "one press of the finger produces long, steady, forceful ring. Ven I am through, yours vill do same!"

"Michael," Mom said, smiling weakly, "I know the bell has been on David's fix-it list for a while, and . . . uh, thank you for repairing it and all, but—"

"My pleasure!" Michael chimed in. "Zis way, when guests come zey don't need to go to back door and scare family as we did last night!"

Mom sighed as Michael headed for the front door again. She wasn't sure what he meant by the phrase, "long, forceful ring," but—

RIIIIIIIIIIIIIIIIIIIIIIIIIIIIIIIIIINNNNNGGGG!

She was getting the idea.

As the sound of the doorbell slowly faded, Ilie skipped down the stairs and into the kitchen. "Good morning, Meesus Martin. Look what I made you." He handed her a large, wooden, hand-carved something-or-other.

Mom was at a loss for words. It was big and intricately carved, but a big and intricately carved *what?* "Uh . . . thank you," she finally said, carefully looking it over for clues.

At last she noticed the safety pin on the back. *A pin,* she thought. *But it's so big . . .*

"You're velcome," Ilie beamed as he stood waiting for her to pin it onto her blouse.

Reluctantly, Mom unlatched the pin and stuck it on. "There," she said forcing her best smile.

"Uh, Meesus Martin," Ilie hesitated, "you've . . . peenned eet upside down."

"Oh, sorry," Mom said in embarrassment as she fumbled to turn it around. "I knew that." At last she pinned it correctly.

Ilie broke into another grin and strolled out of the kitchen with the look of satisfaction spread across his face.

RIIIIIIIIIIIIIIIIIIIIIIIIIIIIIIIIIINNNNNNNNG!

Mom gave another jump—not only at the ring

but at the sight of Nick half-falling, half-stumbling down the stairs. "Will someone answer that door?" he grumbled, still asleep.

Mom sighed.

Nicholas lumbered over to the breakfast table and slung his backpack onto the chair. It was about then he noticed Mom's pin. "I see the Romanian Wood Fiend has struck again," he moaned.

"He made you a gift, too?" Mom asked.

Nicholas unzipped his backpack and pulled out a beautifully carved wooden cup. "I think it's supposed to be a pencil holder," he grumbled. "Who knows."

Mom raised an eyebrow at his tone. "Sounds like someone got up on the wrong side of the cot."

"There is no *right* side to that cot," he mumbled as he poured himself some orange juice. "Even when I stay over at Louis's, his bunk bed isn't that hard."

"Oh, that reminds me," Mom said, "you'd better call Louis and tell him you can't go to the game."

"But Mom!" Nick cried, suddenly wide awake. "This will be the first pro game I see!"

"I'm sorry," Mom said, shaking her head, "but you're Ilie's host. You can't just get up and leave in the middle of his visit. Louis will understand."

Nick was furious. Sleeping on the cot was bad enough, but missing his first pro game because Ilie was visiting . . . well, that was definitely pushing the meaning of "hospitality."

Mom read his thoughts perfectly. "We all have to make sacrifices, dear."

"But why am *I* always the one?" Nick whined.

"I don't think you're the only one," Mom complained. "Thanksgiving dinner is tough enough with your sister sick." She opened the cupboard and began looking for some cans. "But toss in a few last-minute guests, ringing bells, and some 'Romanian Cabbage Casserole,' and—"

Suddenly Ilie and Michael entered the room together.

"Ze bell . . . she ees fixed," Michael announced proudly. He reached up and replaced the box back over the bell. "Next I fix faulty light."

He crossed to the wall switch next to the sink. "Most perplexing. When you turn on switch, instead of light," he flipped on the switch, "out comes terrible rumble from sink."

There was a rumble all right—from the garbage disposal!

"It's all right, Michael," Mom said as she hurried over to turn off the disposal. "It's supposed to do that."

Once again the intercom buzzer sounded.

"Ees someone at ze door?" Michael asked, puzzled that his doorbell was now making a buzzing noise.

"No, that's Jamie," Mom sighed, as she crossed to the intercom.

"Mom," Jamie's voice crackled from the speaker, "you forgot to bring me a spoon for my cereal."

"Sorry . . . "

Jamie continued. "And every time the doorbell rings there's static on the TV."

Michael stooped down to examine the little speaker. "This ees amazing device," he exclaimed.

"Yeah, it keeps me busy," Mom agreed.

"Did we get chocolate milk yet?" Jamie's voice asked.

"Ahhh . . . sorry, sweetie," Mom said. "I forgot."

Michael's smile broadened. "Ilie and me go to store for you! All our lives have we heard tales of American gro-sir-ee stores like we see on TV een 'You Love Lucy'. Fred, Ethel, Lucy, and Rickie go to store and—"

"Well, great," Mom interrupted, trying to hide her impatience. She crossed to her purse and pulled out her billfold. "And get some more cabbage, too. Nick can show you how to get there on his way to school."

"But Mom," Nick whined . . . until he saw her "no-nonsense" look. You know the one. The one your parents use that says, "You can argue with me on some things, but you WILL OBEY me on this one."

Nick sighed. "Sure," he said with a forced shrug, "it's on the way."

Mom started to hand Michael a ten-dollar bill. But he lifted his hand and refused. In Romanian he said, *"Omul ejte ch un porc care nu se mai auce vnapoi unde a locuit."*

Ilie saw the puzzled looks on Mom's and Nick's faces, so he translated for his dad. "Zat ees old Romanian saying: A man ees a swine who denies bacon to his neighbor."

Mom gave a weak, "Thank you," then turned and exchanged "Hoo-Boy!" looks with Nick.

This was definitely going to be *some* Thanksgiving.

The walk to town wasn't bad. It wasn't great, either.

Try as he might to stay cool, Nick found himself

getting a little frustrated with Michael and Ilie. They were constantly stopping and staring at this or pointing at that. It was like they were visiting from another planet.

Then there was their friendliness. I mean, did they have to greet *everybody* they saw?

When they passed a house covered with Thanksgiving decorations both Michael and Ilie burst out laughing. Nick didn't see what was so funny. (He would never have guessed it had anything to do with the funny pilgrims in funny pilgrim clothes and funny pilgrim hats, pointing funny pilgrim rifles at turkeys.)

Then there was the school-crossing guard. Everything was going fine until Michael and Ilie stood at attention and saluted the guy. Nick rolled his eyes and prodded them on across, shrugging sheepishly to the guard.

It seemed the more time they spent together, the more distant Nick felt from Ilie. They'd been closer when they were five thousand miles apart. Now that the guy was here, in person, Nick felt like a tour guide for extraterrestrials. Weird. A friend from halfway around the world comes to visit and suddenly all kinds of things bug you—like the way he looks and talks and walks. OK, like everything.

Finally they reached the business district. Michael and Ilie were totally blown away. They turned around in a circle, slowly taking it all in . . . hardware stores, clothing stores, shoe stores, food stores . . . window displays of everything from vacuum cleaners to computers, tomatoes to toasters, Reeboks to ripsaws.

Nick glanced at his watch. "Well, this is where we split up," he said gratefully. "The grocery store is about a block that away." He turned and pointed up the street. "You can't miss it. I get back from school around two so we can—"

But when he turned back to them, they were gone. "What on earth . . . "

Then he spotted them. They were walking down the alley toward a trash Dumpster. He started after them.

"Guys!" he shouted. "Guys, don't go in there. That's the wrong way!"

Soon it was Nick who felt like an extraterrestrial—like he was the one visiting another world. Back alleys were one place he never went. But, with a deep breath for courage, he stepped in.

Deep, menacing shadows seemed to loom from all sides. Dark, grimy walls towered high above him. Graffiti was everywhere. His foot slipped on a pile of trash and, when he reached down to stop himself from falling, he came up with something slimy and smelly on his hand. A dozen flies swarmed around it. And, of course, there was the smell. . . .

At last he reached Michael and Ilie. They were at the Dumpster. The Dumpster where a large figure slowly rose from inside. The figure of a huge, menacing man in rags. A man known throughout the city.

Crazy Jim!

FOUR
Another World

"Ahh . . . hello!" Michael said. He extended his hand to Crazy Jim like they were next-door buddies. "I am Michael Tinescu and zis ees my son—"

Suddenly he stopped. He realized Crazy Jim was standing in the middle of a garbage Dumpster and figured it might be a good idea to help him out. "Oh, let me assist you . . . "

"Please," Crazy Jim said in his best British accent. "Watch the cuffs."

Nick tugged anxiously at Michael's arm and whispered, "That's Crazy Jim! He's a bum and—"

"A bump?" Michael asked.

Before Nicholas could answer, Crazy Jim suddenly leaped out of the Dumpster. "I prefer the term 'gentleman of reduced means,'" he said as he politely tipped his hat. "James Tilman the Third at your service."

"Sorry Crazy . . . I mean James," Nicholas stuttered. He glanced nervously around. This was not the place he wanted to be. Nor was Crazy Jim a

36

man he wanted to be there with. "We were just, uh . . . we were just leaving."

Nick quickly turned, but Crazy Jim darted in front of him. "A word to the wise," he said as he blocked Nick's way with a battered umbrella. "When escorting out-of-towners about, one would do well to advise them to keep their hands to themselves."

Nick gave a nervous laugh.

But Michael paid no attention. He just resumed babbling to Crazy Jim, like they were old friends. "I am worker in relief organization," he said, pulling out his wallet. "But before, I was steel worker in Brasnov."

"Brasnov?" Crazy Jim asked seriously. "Is that near Akron?"

Michael laughed at what he thought was a joke and slapped Crazy Jim on the back. He pulled out a worn photo from his wallet and showed it to him. "Here ees wife at volunteer aid station, following beeg earthquake. And see, here ees son, Ilie," he said, pointing to another picture. Then he turned to Ilie. ". . . who ees here vis me now."

Crazy Jim looked at the boy, but Michael still wasn't finished. "Tell me," he asked, turning to Nick, "what ees meaning of word, *crazy?*"

Crazy Jim jumped in to explain. "Uh . . . I prefer the Old English definition," he said, smiling . . . "'*Crazy:* possessing enthusiasm or excitement.'"

"Ah, yes," Michael said, suddenly nodding in understanding, "like me!"

Nick could only cough slightly. And then, right

on cue, he saw . . . Jordan Michaels, his athletic buddy, standing at the entrance to the alley.

"Hey, Nick? Is that you?" Jordan yelled as he started to approach. "What are you doing down here?"

"Jordan," Nick pretended to smile. This wasn't exactly the type of occasion you'd invite your friends to, but he decided to make the best of it. "Uh, Jordan . . . this is my friend Ilie Tinescu and his dad, Michael . . . they're from Romania."

"Hello!" Michael answered in his usual enthusiasm. Then, turning to Crazy Jim, he continued, "Zis is my friend, James!"

"A pleasure to make your acquaintance, Master Jordan," Crazy Jim said, again politely tipping his hat.

"Yeah, uh . . . hi," Jordan stammered, completely confused. "Ah, listen Nick, if we don't hurry we're gonna be late for school."

"That's right," Nick said a little too agreeably. "We'd better get going."

"Of course," Michael nodded.

"Good-bye," Ilie added.

"Au revoir." Crazy Jim grinned.

Nick gave a nod, turned, and hurried out of the alley with his friend.

"I can't believe this, Jordan," he whispered. "First, I find out I have to miss a trip to the Colts-Bills game because of these guys, and now I'm on a first-name basis with Crazy Jim! What am I going to do?"

"Hey," Jordan cracked, "maybe Crazy Jim will put them up for you so you can go to the game."

"Very funny!" Nicholas sighed, "very funny." Then, just before they rounded the corner he turned back to the three of them. "Don't forget!" he yelled. "The grocery store is two blocks down the street."

"Ve understand," Michael called as he threw his arm around Crazy Jim.

"Bye, Neeck," Ilie called. "Ve'll see you at home. America ees really amazink!!"

"Yeah," Nick murmured as he turned and walked down the street. All he could think was that this wasn't the America he knew. *Normal* people—*good* people—didn't live in alleys and go through Dumpsters. He wasn't exactly sure where it said that in the Bible, but he figured it must be there someplace.

What he didn't know was that his figuring would change.

Soon.

Very soon.

If Nick had looked down the alley in the other direction, he'd have noticed someone else rummaging through trash cans. But this someone else was no Crazy Jim. Oh, he was dressed almost as poorly as Crazy Jim, and he was sifting through the garbage as carefully as Crazy Jim. But this someone was only ten years old.

His name was Steven.

"All right!" Steven cried as he pulled half a potato out of a can. He checked it over for spoiled spots, then wiped it clean and stuffed it in his sweatshirt pocket next to a scrawny bunch of carrots that were sticking out.

He crossed to another set of trash cans. He opened the first one but immediately slammed it shut again. The smell was just too awful.

The second can was filled mostly with paper. He was about to close it when something caught his eye. He reached inside and came up with a football card.

"Hey!" he cheered, holding one up high. "It's Jim Kelly!"

He rummaged around for more, and finally came up with four others. He carefully wiped them off and started to stuff them into his frayed back pocket when he suddenly heard a voice.

"Well, whaddaya know!"

Steven whirled around. Four boys stood there, all neatly dressed in the latest jeans and coats. They stood blocking the alley—and any chance Steven had to make a run for it.

Steven didn't know any of them personally, but by the smirk on their faces he recognized their species: *Genus Bullicus.*

Better known as "bullies."

For a ten-year-old, Steven could handle himself pretty well. Since his family had lost their house three months ago, he'd learned fast—he'd had to—but there were four of these guys and only one of him. And they were bigger. A lot bigger. Mostly eighth graders, he guessed.

Steven stuffed the last football card into his back pocket and tried to walk past the boys, but they would have none of it.

"A real fashion statement, ain't he," a tall skinny one said as he stepped in front of Steven.

"Yeah, nice threads," another said as he flicked a torn fragment of Steven's sleeve.

"It's the latest thing," the biggest and ugliest said as he grabbed Steven's back pocket and easily ripped it down. "It comes apart in your hand."

Everyone laughed as the football cards fluttered to the ground.

"Come on!" Steven protested, as he bent down to scoop them up.

But the big guy's foot suddenly appeared on top of them. He ground his heel into them and growled, "We don't want you freaks cluttering up our streets. You ruin the neighborhood!"

"We do not!" Steven argued, tugging at the big guy's leg, trying to pull the cards free. "We got as much right here as—"

"You got nothin'!" the big guy shouted as he quickly lifted his foot and kicked Steven. The little guy went rolling and crashing into another set of cans as the rest of the boys broke out laughing.

"You don't got rights, man," the big guy sneered. "'Cause you're garbage. Just more garbage cluttering up our streets."

"That's right," the tall, skinny kid nodded as the group started for Steven again. "My old man says you bums bring property value down and ruin business."

"Yeah," the others agreed.

"That's right," the big guy grumbled. "So you better get outta here."

Steven hesitated.

"GET OUT OF HERE!"

Steven needed no more invitations. Without a word, he jumped to his feet and raced down the alley for all he was worth—but even while he ran there was no missing the tears as they streaked down his dirty cheeks.

FIVE
Sour Grapes

It was cold Wednesday morning. Cold enough to
make everybody look like steam engines as they
walked downtown blowing out little puffs of white
breath. But Dad, who was nice and warm in his
car, barely noticed those walking by as he
squealed around the corner and drove into his
parking spot at the newspaper.

He was late. In fact he'd been late every day that
week. He wasn't sure, but he thought it had something to do with Ilie and Michael. With the way
they loved to talk before breakfast . . . during
breakfast . . . after breakfast . . . and anytime in
between.

Dad raced from his car toward the building. His
overcoat tails billowed behind him like wings. Halfway to the revolving doors, he screeched to a halt.
He whirled around, ran back to his car, grabbed
his briefcase, and started all over again.

He almost made it to the doors when Crazy Jim
suddenly stepped out.

"Greetings, my good man," Jim said cheerfully. He held out his hat like it was a church collection plate. "Mightn't I impose upon you to lighten the burden of one whose misfortune it has been to—"

He stopped as Dad fumbled into his pocket and pulled out a wad of dollar bills and some change.

Crazy Jim's eyes grew big at the sight of the dollars. They grew small at the sight of the single quarter Dad dropped into his hat.

"Genuine coin of the realm," Crazy Jim muttered sarcastically. "Hope it doesn't set ya back." He tipped his hat as Dad moved through the door.

For a brief moment Dad felt guilty, but he quickly dismissed the feeling. After all, he was a busy man with lots of things to do.

Crazy Jim stretched, took a deep breath, and started walking. With his feet on automatic pilot, he slowly made his way into a nearby alley. Before he knew it he was standing underneath a large cross. Below it was a sign that read, "Back Alley Mission and Soup Kitchen."

The mission was always good for a fair breakfast, but today there was an extra little attraction. Besides the usual collection of tattered people standing in front of the door, there was a father and son playing a mandolin and singing Romanian folk songs. A father and son who looked exactly like Michael and Ilie.

And with good reason. They *were* Michael and Ilie!

Actually Michael was the one doing the singing and playing. Ilie was passing around a pink bakery box full of pastries and donuts. It wasn't the lowest calorie breakfast these homeless folks had ever had, but who was counting calories? Not these guys. By the looks of things it had been a long time since they had to worry about having too much to eat.

Back at the Martin house things were getting pretty hectic. By afternoon, the kitchen looked like a food factory. Grandma was peeling yams, and Mom was spending more time with cabbage than she had ever dreamed possible.

Ilie, who had finally left the mission, was now pursuing a brand new project. He charged into the kitchen shouting excitedly, "My friends, I vant you all to meet Julia!"

A nice-looking girl in her twenties appeared in the doorway.

Mom pushed a stray curl out of her eyes and looked up. With the room dripping in steam from the bubbling foods and her hands dripping with cabbage juice, it was not a good time for meeting new people. But this new person was a little different. She wore a uniform—a mail carrier's uniform.

"Julia has been bringing letters and packages to zis house for months," Ilie continued, "but she has *never met ze people inside!* Can you believe eet?"

"Oh really?" Mom said, trying to sound surprised.

Actually, it wasn't all that surprising. People live in houses. Mail carriers bring them mail. No biggie. Sure, they might nod at each other in passing, but they don't usually sit down and have tea together . . . (not unless they live in old "Andy Griffith" show reruns). It wasn't anything personal, it was just the way things tended to be in our fast-paced society.

It was clear Julia was feeling a little awkward about the situation. She fidgeted and cleared her throat. "Ah, I usually don't, you know, meet a lot of the people on my route, but Ilie here was so insistent that—"

"She vas telling me about your Thanksgiving holiday!" Ilie interrupted. "It's amazink!"

"Oh? Do you have big plans?" Grandma asked Julia.

"Not really," Julia shrugged. "My roommate and I will probably cook up a bird in the microwave and watch reruns of the parade on TV."

"How . . . lovely," Grandma answered a little uncertainly. "I guess Thanksgiving isn't quite the event it used to be." She wiped her hands and came out from behind the counter. "When I was a child my mother used to have the whole family over . . . and neighbors, too."

Grandma sat on a stool, smiling. "You've never seen so much food: turkey and stuffing, potatoes and gravy, fresh biscuits . . . " Her voice sadly trailed off.

"That sounds really nice," Julia said, trying to picture it.

"Suddenly I am hungry!" Ilie laughed.

Mom smiled as she returned to her Romanian cabbage casserole. "Thanksgiving is more than just big family meal," she said to Ilie. "It's a celebration of the time our forefathers gave thanks to

God for all he had given them. It's a time of sharing your own good fortune with others."

For a moment it sounded like Mom was giving a sermon. But, even as the words came out of her mouth, she was thinking things like, *I wish all these people would leave so I could get back to work,* and, *These holidays are killing me,* and, *Where did I put that soup strainer?*

So much for "sharing your own good fortune with others." You see, like Nicholas, Mom had forgotten a little bit about the spirit of Thanksgiving.

After another awkward moment of silence Julia shifted her mailbag and said, "Well, it's been nice meeting you, but I'd better be getting back to my route."

"Nice meeting you, Julia," Grandma said, still smiling.

Mom, however, was too busy with her work to smile. "Ilie, would you please show Julia out?" she asked as she stuck her head into the cupboard.

"Yes, I would!" Ilie answered brightly. "Come Julia!" he said as he grabbed her hand and practically yanked her toward the door.

Suddenly, the new intercom buzzed.

"Mom," Jamie's voice whined, "Whatever ate my crackers!"

"Now it's the *dog,*" Mom sighed. "I'm not going to make it." She wearily plopped down a box of bread crumbs on the counter and reached for the button.

Ya think ol' Mom was in a bad mood, you should've been around when Nicky boy came home from school. Then again, maybe you shouldn't have.

Then again, maybe I shouldn't have. 'Course, I don't have much choice in the matter. As an imaginary character, I kinda have to go wherever Nick's imagination goes. It's in my contract.

Anyway, Nick knew this was the day he'd have to call Louis and cancel going to that football game. The kid was definitely bummed . . . big time.

But not me. No-siree-bob. I was up on his drawing table building my world-famous "Spy-Tracking Globule"—the preferred globule of spy trackers everywhere. (Don't ask me why we call it a "globule." Probably 'cause it looks like a wad of bubble gum with wires sticking out every which way. But there was a good reason it looked like that. It WAS a wad of bubble gum with wires sticking out every which way.)

Anyhoo, I still didn't buy the idea that Michael and his boy blunder were do-gooders who'd come to America to help. Who did they think they were kidding? I know top-secret Soviet spies when I see them. And this Spy-Tracking Globule would help me see them . . . anywhere . . . day or night.

I continued my last-minute adjustments on the marvelous maze of merchandise as Nick dialed up Indianapolis and began his little "Whine Time" with Louis. "I've tried everything," he moaned into the phone, "but I'm stuck here, baby-sitting my friend from Romania and his fath—"

That's all I remember. Suddenly my incredibly intuitive inventive invention ignited. (Translation for you younger readers:

It blowed up and goed big boom.)

The room was filled with more smoke than the

*boy's lavatory at lunchtime. I was fried faster than
a fly in a bug zapper.*

*And the Spy-Tracking Globule? Rumor has it, it
was raining bubble gum as far away as Toledo.*

It was back to the drawing board . . . literally.

As McGee went back to work, Nick remained on
the phone complaining to Louis.

"I mean, Ilie and I just don't have anything in
common." He plopped down on his bed with the
phone stuck to his ear and continued. "His idea of
fun is hanging out with street people. And you
wouldn't believe what he just brought home—our
mail girl!"

Nick toyed with the wooden cup Ilie had made
him as he grumbled on. "He was OK as a pen pal,
but he's just too much of a Dweeb-O-Matic to be
in the same country with." He took aim at the
trash can and tossed the cup across the room.

Nicholas didn't pay much attention to the cup
after it left his hand.

Someone else, however, noticed the cup right
away. Ilie had just come down the hall and was
about to enter Nick's room when he saw the cup
bounce off the trash can and roll across the floor.

Then he heard Nick's voice: "I just wish Ilie and
his dad had never come."

Ilie's nonstop smile suddenly stopped. He tried
to swallow back the lump that quickly formed in
his throat, but it did no good. Then there was the
burning in his eyes. He did his best to blink back

the tears, but with little success. Finally he turned and headed back down the hall toward the stairs.

A couple of seconds later Nick finished his conversation with Louis. He hung up with the world's longest sigh just as Mom whisked in. She looked even more frayed than before as she carried a tray of dirty dishes from Jamie's room.

"Do you have Jamie's Walkman?" she asked.

"Yeah," Nicholas said. "Ilie was using it over by the art table." Then, making sure his voice dripped with sarcasm, he continued, "It was, of course, 'amazink.'"

Mom turned to him. "What's wrong with Ilie, anyway?" she asked.

"Do you want the long list or the short list?" Nick muttered as he plopped back down on his bed.

"No, I mean now," Mom said as she glanced toward the door. "He looked pretty upset. I just passed him outside your door, and he didn't say a word."

A look of panic flashed across Nick's face. He lurched up from his bed. *"What?!"* In a flash he was off the bed and rushing to look up and down the hallway.

Ilie was nowhere in sight.

Seconds later Nick was tumbling down the staircase and into the family room . . . just as Sarah entered through the door.

"Sarah," he cried, grabbing her by the shoulders. "Have you seen Ilie?!"

"Well, yeah," she said, looking a little startled. "He and his dad just left."

"What?!" Nick yelped. He turned and raced for the door.

"I was coming in," Sarah continued, "and they left. Funny thing is, they were carrying their suitcase."

Nick barely heard her as he flung open the screen door and raced outside. But neither Ilie nor Michael were in view.

A sick feeling welled up in Nick's stomach. He was sure now that Ilie had heard his conversation with Louis.

And he knew the boy and his father were leaving . . .

And he knew whose fault it was.

SIX
Missing Persons

Nicky boy had really blown it. Big time. And, as usual, it was up to me to unblow it—bigger time. Yes-siree-bob, somebody had to find Ilie and Michael. Somebody with brains, humility, and good looks—and let's not forget the great hair—but in addition to all those amazingly awesome attributes, it had to be somebody with a new and improved . . . Spy-Tracking Globule.

That's right. My little gizmo was finally up and working. Already it had answers to such questions as, How come kids can chew gum at home but not at school? Why do Moms hate to see their sons lying around the house when there are leaves to rake? And, most important, Why do cats always use their litter box just as soon as you've emptied it?

But that was small potatoes compared to the real question at hand: Where were Ilie and Michael?

At the moment, I was hidden away in my handy-dandy traveling spy laboratory—better known as

Nick's coat pocket. Here I dialed dials, switched switches, and knobbed knobs.

Suddenly I heard it:

Beep-beep-beep-(burp) . . .

The beeps were my machine locking onto its target. (The burp was one too many cans of Diet Dr. Pepper.)

Nicholas opened his coat pocket, looked inside, and, in his best whine, complained, "McGee, this is never going to work. We'll never find Ilie and his dad."

"What are you talking about?" I cried. "Can't you hear the beeping? The Tracking Globule glob that I stuck on their suitcase is sending out the signal!"

"McGee . . . "

I guess the kid was a little doubtful about the machine's accuracy. So far we'd tracked down a giant bank building, an '84 Oldsmobile, and . . . a fire hydrant.

Amazing! What a device! What an inventor! Who else could have found such objects? . . . I mean, I'll bet no one even knew they were missing in the first place! Now, if that's not genius, I'd like to know what is.

"C'mon, trust me," I insisted, "we'll find them in no time."

Suddenly the beeps grew louder.

"See? What'd I tell you!" I shouted. "We got 'em! They're just around that corner! Hurry!"

Reluctantly Nick started to run. We reached the corner, raced around it, and ran smack-dab into:

WHOOOOAAAA . . . CRASH!

. . . Julia, the mail lady.

We knocked that babe flatter than a football playing chicken with a semi. There were more stars circling her head than Academy Award night in Hollywood.

Nick and I were also on the ground. He was a little dazed, but not me. One of the nice things about being a cartoon character is that when you get flattened, you always pop back up as good as new for the next scene.

Nick scrambled to his feet. Julia, however, wasn't quite so fast. In fact, she was still lying on the sidewalk stretched out in a thick pool of . . . a thick pool of . . . ENVELOPES! (Ah-HA! You thought I was going to say blood, didn't you? I tell ya, you've got to stop watching all that violence on TV. In fact, I know this great video series about a kid with an imaginary cartoon friend who is incredibly handsome and . . . well, never mind, we'll talk about that some other time.)

Immediately Nicholas was offering Julia his hand. "Sorry about that," he said with more than a little embarrassment.

"That's OK," she said, with more than a little wobbling. "Occupational hazard."

"You haven't by any chance seen Ilie have you?" Nick asked as he helped her pick up the scattered envelopes. "You know, the boy who—"

"How could I forget?" Julia chuckled as she swung her bag across her shoulder. "Thanks to him I'm on a first-name basis with everyone in the neighborhood, including their cats and dogs."

Nicholas tried to laugh. Of course she wasn't as

clever and witty as me, but you couldn't fault her for trying.

She shook her head. "I haven't seen Ilie since I left your house. I'll keep an eye out for him though."

"Thanks," Nick said as he handed her the last of the envelopes.

She nodded and started back down the street. She was still a little wobbly but was basically heading in the right direction.

Nick sighed and glared down into his pocket at me.

"Hey," I yelled. "Don't look at me in that tone of voice!"

"'They're just around the corner,'" he mocked. "Sure thing, McGee."

I gave kind of a sheepish shrug and confessed, "I guess my Tracking Globule needs a little, uh . . . re-globulating."

With the Tracking Globule now history, Nick expanded his search into the business district. He even swung by Dad's office building and later checked the Dumpster where they had run into Crazy Jim.

No Ilie . . . No Michael . . . For that matter, no Crazy Jim, either.

Nick began stopping people on the street and asking them if they'd seen Michael and Ilie. Again, no response . . . unless you count the old lady who clobbered him with her umbrella 'cause she thought he was a mugger.

By the time evening rolled around, Nick had given up hope. He slowly trudged home. His feet were killing him, but that was nothing compared to the pain in the middle of his chest.

At that exact moment somebody else was trudging home. . . .

It was dark under the freeway bridge as Steven found the hole in the chain link fence and squeezed through. He began running. He had to. His mom had expected him hours ago.

Cars and trucks rumbled overhead as he passed one giant freeway pylon after another. Finally he came upon their old station wagon. Next to it was a collection of refrigerator boxes and pieces of cardboard that made up his family's home.

At least, they *called* it home . . . because that's where they lived. But everyone else would say they were homeless, because a car and a bunch of boxes was no place for anybody to live.

Still, it had been a good day for Steven. He had managed to hit a McDonald's Dumpster twice at just the right time. That meant he not only had plenty of half-eaten Breakfast Burritos, but lots of pieces of Quarter Pounders and Chicken McNuggets, too.

"It's Stevie!" his two little sisters called as he poked his head inside the cardboard. "Mom! It's Stevie!"

They jumped up and greeted him. Of course, it wasn't just him they were interested in. It was also the sack he carried and whatever surprises he might have found and stuffed in his pockets for them. Why, just yesterday he'd brought back a rubber dinosaur and a small stuffed penguin.

"Whatcha got? Whatcha got?" they asked, digging into his pockets and reaching for the sack.

"Go away!" he shouted, shaking them off. "I got no toys today, just food."

"Where have you been?" his mother demanded. There was no missing the fear in her voice.

Steven looked up and swallowed. She hovered over him, glowering.

"I've been gettin' . . . stuff," he said, holding out the McDonald's sack to her. "I had to swing by the college snack bar to microwave it to kill all the germs."

She snatched the sack out of his hand. "You're supposed to be home before dark. You know that! There's all sorts of ugly people out there. What if . . . " Suddenly her voice started to crack. "What if . . . " She could no longer continue. She could only reach out and pull him into her arms. So much for anger. Now, it was a time for tears.

"I'm sorry, Mom . . . "

"I-I know it's . . . hard," she stammered, pressing her cheek against his head. "I know you want to do all you can to help. But you . . . you've got to be more careful . . . you've *got* to!"

She held him for a long moment—almost like she was afraid to let him go. Finally she released him. "Now go wash up," she ordered, straightening herself and wiping her eyes. She turned to her two daughters, pretending nothing had happened. "Girls, help me set the table."

They grumbled and complained as they stepped outside and washed their hands in the plastic paint bucket they refilled each day from a local fire hydrant.

Outside, Steven noticed his dad sitting in a folding lawn chair. He was by a little fire, staring into the flames. It was dangerous having a fire. If some official saw it, he could run the family off again. But they had no choice. It would get down to freezing again tonight, and they needed the heat.

"How'd it go?" Steven asked as he joined his dad and warmed his hands.

The man let out a slow sigh as he wrapped his arm around Steven's waist. "No job . . . not yet."

Steven nodded. His dad had changed a lot over the months. But what hurt Steven the most was his jokes. Or, actually, the lack of them. A year ago his dad had had a joke for everything. True, most of them were groaners, but they'd been fun to listen to. Now . . . well, let's just say Steven missed the jokes the most.

"I didn't do too bad," Steven said trying to sound cheery. "I got some food and, look." He pulled a compass out of his pocket. "I found this so we won't get lost."

"That's fine, Stevie," his dad said, patting him on the shoulder. "I can always count on you." He threw a quick glance toward Steven's mom, who had also stepped outside. He pulled his son closer and whispered, "But don't be gone so long anymore . . . for Mom's sake. She was pretty worried."

"I'm sorry," Steven said.

A long moment of silence hung between the two. Finally Steven spoke again. "Dad . . . tomorrow's Thanksgiving, isn't it?"

"Yes," the man answered quietly.

"Are we gonna do anything, you know, special for it?"

His dad stared back into the fire. "Maybe . . . I don't know. At the moment we're a little short on things to be thankful for."

Then, without a word, the man rose and took a few steps away. He was either examining the darkness or trying to keep his son from seeing his tears. It wasn't hard to guess which.

Finally he sighed and turned back to Steven. "I guess we do have a few things to be thankful for. At least we're all together." With that he turned and headed for the table.

Actually, "the table" was just another large box on its side. Steven's mom had set out some old plastic plates. On them were scattered pieces of Steven's take from McDonald's.

"Dad?" Steven asked as they sat down. "I met this strange man today. He had a beard and—"

"I told you never to speak to strangers," his mother interrupted.

"I didn't say a word," Steven insisted. "But he handed this to me." He took off his shoe and pulled out a ten-dollar bill from inside.

Everyone stared in amazement.

"A stranger gave that to you?" his mom asked.

"Yeah," Steven said, nodding. "And then he disappeared into the crowd—almost like he was a ghost or something."

His mom took the money. "A ghost?" she grinned. "Pretty rich for a ghost."

"Maybe he was an angel!" the oldest sister cried.

"He was real nice," Steven said. "Didn't say a word 'till the end, and then it was kinda strange."

"What'd he say that was so strange?" his mom asked.

"He said, 'Trust God . . . you're not alone.'"

"Probably one of those religious fanatics bribing you to believe in God," his dad said with a loud snort. "God . . . there is no God! Not for us." He paused for a moment, then said, "But he's right about one thing. We're not alone—we got each other."

Steven glanced up at his dad, then to his mom. Finally he looked to the beams of moving light that spilled down from the freeway over their heads. His dad was right. They weren't alone, they did have each other.

But somehow, Steven suspected that the stranger meant more than that. A lot more. . . .

SEVEN
Spy-Tracker

Back at home, Nick felt pretty low. He put on his pajamas then sat (more like drooped) at his art table. He stared vacantly at his drawing pad. Maybe if he doodled something . . . put ol' McGee into an adventure, maybe then he could pull himself out of this slump.

He picked up his pencil, but it felt like a lead brick. Not a good sign. Then his eyes fell on the cup Ilie gave him. It was still on the floor where he'd thrown it when Ilie had run away.

Nicholas crossed over and picked it up. Once again he looked at its intricate designs. *All that carving must've taken Ilie a long time,* he thought. Finally Nick noticed an inscription on the bottom:

"To Nick, my best American friend . . . Ilie."

As if that wasn't bad enough, Nicholas spotted something else. Just below the inscription were more letters. Painted. He pronounced the syllables out loud as he put them together. "Car . . . paith . . . ia."

He repeated the name, almost shouting, *"Carpaithia!"*

Nicholas's stomach dropped to the floor. Ilie had made the pencil cup out of his prized model ship! The one he had talked about when they were examining Nick's red glider.

It was a low blow. The lowest. And Nicholas knew he'd given it to himself.

"Man . . . ," he groaned. "I really messed up."

Suddenly I popped up out of the drawing pad. "Yeah," I said, trying to sound sympathetic. "Now you know how a turkey feels on Thanksgiving."

OK, OK, so I'm not the world's most sympathetic friend, but with my terrific looks, sparkling personality, and perfectly straight teeth . . . let's face it, I'm still as close to perfection as they come, right?

I said, "RIGHT?"

HEY! IS ANYBODY OUT THERE??

I tell ya, for a reader, you're not the most talkative person I've ever met. I guess my greatness can be kinda intimidating sometimes, right?

I said, "RIGHT?"

Oh, forget it.

Nicholas was about to give up, too. "I didn't even give Ilie a chance," he said. "All I could think of was my own, stupid self and that stupid football game." He set the cup down on the table and stared at it. "Now I'll probably never see Ilie again."

"Don't be so sure," I said. "I know a guy who can find anybody."

"Oh, yeah? Who's that?" Nick looked to me suspiciously.

It was now or never. Although I'd known Nicky boy for years it was time to share my deepest secret. Time to reveal my true identity. Yes, believe it or not, I wasn't just a superiorly gorgeous hunk of cartoon creativity. That was only a cover, a clever disguise to protect my true identity.

Quicker than you can say, "Oh no! Are we about to do another McGee fantasy?" I whipped out a pair of sunglasses, slid them on, and spoke in my best British accent:

"The name's Blond . . . James Blond."

"Oh, brother," Nick groaned. "McGee, please, I'm not in the mood. . . ."

But he was too late. Already the drawing table was turning into some sleazy street on the sleazy side of the tracks in the sleaziest section of some sleazy European city. You could tell it was in Europe because the police sirens didn't go RRRRRRRRRRrrrrrr . . . ; they went "Bleeeh-Blaaaah, Bleeeh-Blaaah, Bleeeh-Blaaah."

With the suave elegance, cool detachment, and wry humor only British superspies can use effectively, I pursued my archnemesis, Dimitri Villinov, through the back sleazy streets.

Suddenly a sleazy guy (I think I've used the word sleazy enough, don't you?) in a sleazy trench coat (OK, OK, I promise. No more.) disappeared around a sleaz—uh, a dark and sinister corner.

Quickly I pulled out my incredible Spy-Tracking Globular Device and (since this is a fantasy) it worked perfectly.

Beep . . . Beep . . . Beep . . .

I was hot on his trail. Like a shadow. Step for

step, turn for turn. Any minute and I'd have this notorious, no-good, not-so-nice guy in custody. Just a few more steps and . . .

WOOOOOOAAAHHHHHHH!

That is obviously the sound of someone falling through an open manhole. An open manhole that drops into a sewer.

SPLAAAAAAASHHHHH!

No need to describe that sound.

But this was no ordinary sewer. No way. We're talking your big-time, state-of-the-smell, Toxic Waste Sewer.

But never one to lose my cool or dirty my dinner jacket, I activated my portable All-Purpose-Gadget-ron. Quickly I pressed a button on my wrist and . . .

Zoing! Snap, Click, Click, Click—AOOOOGAA!

It completely surrounded me and unfolded into a one-man submarine. (What I won't think of next, huh?) Being an expert submarine pilot, I carefully steered my craft through the gunk and back up to the surface.

But that is not the end. Oh no, dear reader. Flip ahead and you'll see we still have several more pages to go.

Once out of the obnoxiously odious ooze, the All-Purpose-Gadgetron changed into . . .

Zoing!—Snap, Click, Click, Click—VAROOM, VAROOM!

. . . A jet-powered motorcycle.

I hopped aboard, zoomed out of the alley, and back onto the street. As luck would have it there was Villinov straight ahead. The dastardly criminal was carrying two packages into a nearby building.

They were either plastic explosives or Girl Scout Cookies (sometimes it's hard to tell the difference). Fearing the worst, I roared toward the door.

Unfortunately, a big-rig truck was also roaring . . . right at your beloved hero! Would this be it? Would this be my last caper? Would I go the route of Maxwell Smart and all the other great spies—lost forever in Nickelodeon reruns?

Fear not. There was still one last button on my Gadgetron. With the blinding speed of a touch typist, I punched the key. Suddenly . . .

ZOING!—Snap, Click, Click, Click—ROOOOAR, WOOOSH!

. . . the cycle turned into a rocket-powered hang glider. Just before I and the eighteen-wheeler become inseparable buddies, I roared high into the air, out of harm's way.

Now, flying above the street, I spied Villinov's silhouette through a fifteenth-story window, along with a bunch of other silhouettes. Obviously there was a secret meeting of totally tasteless and terrible troublemakers in the making. I banked my glider and zoomed in. Seconds later I exploded through the window and sent the main man flying across the room.

"Hope I'm not crashing your party?" I said smoothly.

"Thatza exactly what you'vea done!" the man sneered in an Italian accent.

Great Scott! I had created one of history's greatest moments. Yes, believe it or not, the great me had actually made a mistake. It was not Villinov, the Soviet's greatest secret spy. It was Guido, your average, run-of-the-mill pizza delivery guy.

And the other members of his secret meeting were not members of anything. They were all astonished partygoers, holding little wiener thingies on toothpicks and staring at me.

Uh-ohhh . . .

They began to complain, then yell, then wave their toothpicks menacingly at your true-blue hero. Before becoming their next appetizer, I apologized— "So sorry, old chaps"—and prepared to leave.

But not before helping myself to a nearby tray of drinks. "Ahh, Chateau Co-lah '93—shaken, not stirred." I announced as I grabbed a pop can, shook it, and popped it open.

Unfortunately, fizz showered over everyone. Suddenly they were all soaked. Really soaked. Not only were they soaked, but they were steamed.

"GET HIM!" they screamed.

The entire crowd began chasing me around the banquet table. Guido thought he'd join in the fun, too, by throwing one pizza after another at me.

Suddenly I heard laughing. Well, not really laughing, but smiling. OK, so I didn't hear smiling, I saw it. The point is my little fantasy was dissolving. Before I knew it I was standing back on the art table. I glanced over to Nick. His mood had definitely lightened. . . .

"Thanks for the thought," he chuckled as he reached for the light. "But I think this is one mystery I'll have to solve on my own."

The light went out.

But not before a pizza the size of the national

debt flew in from the sketchpad and nailed me in the kisser.

"Hooo-Hooo-Hooo," somebody laughed in an Italian accent. (I just hate smart-aleck fantasies that don't know when to end, don't you?)

"McGee?" Nick asked from his bed. "Did you say something?"

"Naw," I grumbled as I pulled the stringy pizza from my face. "I'm just having a little bedtime snack."

The next morning Thanksgiving blew in, cold and windy. At least it wasn't snowing. Of course, that disappointed all the kids with sleds and cozy fireplaces. But for Steven and his family it was a relief. Cardboard doesn't hold up well under snow.

Unfortunately, the weather was about the only good thing that morning. Holidays meant empty fast-food Dumpsters . . . which meant empty stomachs. Steven had been out on the streets all morning and had found nothing.

Still, he couldn't shake the feeling that something good was going to happen. He remembered the man who had given him the ten dollars. He could still picture the look of kindness in his eyes. He could still hear the voice: "Trust God . . . you're not alone."

What did he mean? Was he an angel? Who was he talking about? God?

Eventually Steven found himself in front of a restaurant. It was torture. Besides the incredible smells, the windows were painted with pictures to advertise their Thanksgiving Dinner Special. Pictures of turkey and dressing, sweet potatoes, and pies piled high with whipped cream.

Steven leaned his forehead against the window and peered in. Inside there were dining tables, a long soup and salad bar, and double doors that swung open and shut as serving people brought out trays of food. Any minute the restaurant would be open for business. Any minute he might be able to—

Suddenly a large face appeared in the window before him. Steven jumped in fright.

"Get away from here!" the muffled voice cried from behind the glass. "Get away or I'm calling the cops!"

Steven turned and walked quickly down the street. His eyes started to smart with tears. His anger burned. "I'm no thief," he muttered. "Can't a guy even look?" Again he thought of the man with the ten dollars. Again he remembered what he had said. *"You are not alone."*

Ha! Who was the man kidding? Steven *was* alone. All alone! There was no angel. There was no God. There was just him. Alone.

Then he heard something. At first he couldn't make it out. He wiped his eyes and followed the sound into a nearby alley.

Somebody was singing—lots of somebodies.

It grew louder and louder. Finally, he spotted the door with a cross above it. Several people stood in front singing and warmly greeting other people.

It's a mission, Steven thought. He'd heard about them. His mom and dad had told him to stay away

68

from them. His shoulders sagged as he turned back . . . until a friendly voice from behind cried, "Hello!"

Steven whirled around to see a boy his size standing with a grocery sack full of bread loaves. "Vould you like to come eenside?" the boy asked brightly.

As you may have guessed, this was no ordinary boy. This was Ilie. In spite of Nick's harsh words, Ilie still hadn't lost his sparkle.

Steven looked at him a moment, then he shook his head. "No, thanks," he said. "My mom told me not to go into . . . places like that."

"Why?" Ilie looked puzzled. "It costs you nothing and—"

"Look, I don't know," Steven said, backing away. "It's just that . . . well, we won't join your . . . uh . . . group just for a handout."

"Oh!" Ilie nodded. "I see. Zat's what your parents told you, eh?"

"Yeah . . . uh . . . now I have to get home and . . ." He turned to leave.

"But eets not like that at all," Ilie called to him. "We just want to help. Jesus healed and fed and helped people, and he told us to do ze same. He cares, so we care, too."

Steven turned back to Ilie. Was this guy for real? Where were the strings? What did he *really* want?

Ilie continued. "And, since we believe Jesus ees greatest gift of all, you can't blame us for we want to share him with you. After all," he said, "you are not alone."

Steven froze. There was that phrase again. The

same one the man who gave him the money had used. Not only that, but as Steven looked into Ilie's eyes, he saw the same expression he had seen on the man's face: a look of kindness mixed with joy and love. It was eerie, but Steven knew it was no accident. He hesitated, unsure.

"Come inside. I show you," Ilie said, gesturing toward the mission. Then he leaned in and whispered, "Besides, ze food ees terrific. I help cook it myself." He winked and Steven smiled.

The two of them started toward the door, then Steven suddenly stopped. "What about my family?" he asked. "I should go get them."

"Come eenside, first," Ilie said, "then you will have more to tell them when you go get them."

Again Steven smiled. He couldn't help it. Something about Ilie's joy was contagious.

They went up to the door, past the singers, past Michael, who was grinning and playing his mandolin . . . and they finally stepped inside.

EIGHT
A Day for Turkeys

Over in Nicholas's neighborhood it was pretty much Thanksgiving as usual. Leaves fluttered from the sky like red and yellow confetti. The backyard Nick had raked so carefully a couple of days earlier was already covered in a thick new carpet.

And inside . . . inside it was your typical "pre–Thanksgiving dinner craziness." The TV blared with parades (and cartoon-character balloons the size of Kansas). And then there was football. Lots of football. Lots and lots of football.

But not for the womenfolk. No sir. To the women, football was peanuts! Mom, Sarah, and Grandma had their own Olympic-type of athletics going as they ran around the kitchen madly preparing the dinner.

"I can't believe Michael and Ilie took off like that," Mom muttered as she poked her head in the oven to check on the bread.

About this time Jamie's intercom buzzed.

Mom jerked up to answer but forgot to pull her head out of the oven first.

BAM!

(If you thought that sounded like a mother's head hitting the top of an oven, you're right.)

"Mom," Jamie's voice whined through the intercom. "How soon is dinner? I'm hungry! Can you bring me something to eat?"

"I'll see what I can do," Mom answered, rubbing her head. She glanced at all the food on the counter. "We have enough to feed the entire Marine Corps. I'm sure we can find you something."

Grandma crossed from the table, looking a little harried. "What shall I do with the Romanian Cabbage Casserole?"

"Put it on the table," Mom said, heading for the pantry. "After all that work, we're at least going to try it." She snatched some crackers and cheese spread and started for Jamie's room.

Meanwhile, Nicholas was up in his room feeling about as worthless as used dental floss. On a scale of one to ten, his self-esteem was about .0000000000001.

When Mom walked in, he was lying on his bed, staring up at his glider.

"Nick, come on downstairs," she said with a sigh. "We're almost ready."

But Nicholas didn't move. "I'm not hungry," he murmured with the enthusiasm of a drugged zombie.

"Not hungry?" she playfully scorned as she crossed over to him. "I fixed enough food for an

army! And with Ilie and Michael gone, I'm counting on *you* to at least eat the cabbage casserole!"
She poked her finger at his ribs.

But Nick didn't smile. He barely moved. He just
lay there, his eyes focused on intergalactic nothing-
ness. "I really messed up, didn't I?" he mumbled.
"He was my friend and I treated him like . . . "

"We all did," Mom said as she took a deep
breath. "Sometimes life starts moving so fast that
we forget to love others. We think only of our-
selves."

"I'm really sorry . . . "

Again Mom sighed. "So am I, honey, so am I."

A half hour later the family was gathered around
the dining table. With all the extra extension
leaves put into it, the table was about the size of
an aircraft carrier. (And with all the food piled on
top of it, it also weighed about as much as a carrier.)

Everyone wore their best duds. When they sat
down, though, two seats were still empty—Jamie's
(thanks to the measles) and Dad's (thanks to the
football game still on the tube).

"David!" Mom called.

But Dad didn't hear. His team was down by a
field goal and there was only one minute to go.
Perched on the edge of his seat, his eyes wide, his
adrenaline pumping, Dad watched as the announcer shouted, "He's at the forty! . . . the thirty!!
. . . the—"

Suddenly the screen went blank.

"What? Hey!" Dad exploded . . . until he saw

Mom holding the remote. One look at her face told him this was not the time to protest. The meal had been three days in the making and would take another three days to clean up. It was going to be eaten when it was hot *or Mom's name wasn't Mom!*

Dad swallowed nervously. "Not waiting on me, I hope?" he asked sheepishly as he crossed to the table and took his seat.

After everyone got settled, Dad turned to his son and asked, "Nicholas, will you give thanks for us?"

"Me?" Nick looked up in surprise. The last thing he wanted to do was pray. After what he'd pulled, who was he to pray for anything or anybody?

Dad nodded for him to go ahead.

The family took one another's hands and, reluctantly, Nick bowed his head. It took a moment for the words to come. "I'm thankful," he croaked, "that I, uh . . . had a friend like Ilie. And maybe, with your help, he'll be able to . . . forgive me for what I did."

Nick paused a moment as if searching his thoughts.

Sarah coughed slightly to remind him she'd like to eat before Christmas.

Finally, he continued. "Bless him . . . and bless this food. Amen."

For a moment Nick didn't look up. Then he felt the squeeze of understanding coming from Mom's hand. He looked over to her, and she smiled. He tried to return it.

"All right," Grandma said as she reached for the mashed potatoes and started to pass them. "Let's get this meal on the road."

Suddenly there was a loud knock at the window.

Everyone jumped and turned toward it. The last time this had happened it had been in the middle of the night and the mystery knockers had been Michael and Ilie. This time it was the middle of the day and it was . . . Michael and Ilie!!

Nicholas leaped from his seat and raced toward the door.

"Theyyyy're baaaacckkk!" Sarah announced ominously.

Nick flung open the back door. He couldn't believe it. There they were, just like on the first night. God was giving him another chance!

"No answer to bell," Michael said with a shrug, "so we come to back." They stepped gingerly inside as though nothing had gone wrong—as though the last twenty-four hours had never happened.

"I thought . . . I . . . " Nick stammered, confused. "Where were you guys?!"

Michael and Ilie exchanged puzzled looks as the rest of the family rose to join them.

"Didn't you get note?" Michael asked, rummaging through his pockets. "I am sure I left note for you. . . ." He pulled a crumpled piece of paper from his pocket. " . . . een my own pocket?" he finished weakly.

Everyone chuckled.

"My friends, please forgive me," he said with an embarrassed look. "Yesterday, Ilie and I, we go to Back Alley Mission to help feed peoples who have not enough food and—"

"You've been doing volunteer work all this time?" Dad interrupted.

Ilie nodded in excitement.

"Please," Dad said, gesturing to the table, "grab a chair and join us."

Michael obeyed wholeheartedly. "So many peoples to feed," he said with a sigh, "and so few to help feed them. We like to do what we could, to share what we have, just like Meesus Martin said."

"Like I said?" Mom asked in surprise.

"Yes, Meesus Martin," Ilie agreed. For some reason he was still at the window looking outside. "Before, een kitchen, when I hear you tell Julia, ze mail carrier, how Thanksgiving ees a time of sharing good fortune with others, I think then you are very wise."

"So, een suitcase," Michael continued, "we bring clothes to share with those who have not enough to wear."

"You gave away your clothes?" Nick asked in amazement. He didn't know what it was like in Romania, but around here you were what you wore. To give up your clothes was like giving up a piece of yourself.

"Ah, but we also receive!" Michael exclaimed, holding up Crazy Jim's tattered hat. "Just like Indiana Jones, no?"

"More like Indiana James," Nick said, taking the rumpled hat from him and looking it over.

Suddenly Ilie had spotted what he was looking for. "Papa, they are coming!"

"Who are coming?!" Mom asked, glancing from one to the other. There was no missing the hint of concern crossing her face.

Ilie opened the door and called out, "Back here everybody!"

"I will explain," Michael said, walking over to Mom. "As you say, we eenvite people we meet—neighbors, friends . . . "

"You invited . . . people?" Mom asked, her concern turning to dismay.

"No worries," Michael reassured her. "Knowing of Meesus Martin's spirit of giving, I say to pastor at mission, 'I know where to send extra peoples when mission run out of room.'"

"Oh, Michael," Mom said with a panicked look, "I wish I'd known sooner . . ."

"Did someone mention food?" a voice called from the doorway. Everyone looked. Crazy Jim sauntered inside. In his hands was a foil-covered turkey the size of the Goodyear blimp. Behind him were a couple of mission workers carrying boxes of paper plates, utensils, and roasting pans full of even more food.

Mom smiled in relief, then moved into action. She quickly cleared the counter and the table to make a buffet area.

Meanwhile, Grandma and Sarah went to work laying out the plates and utensils.

Nick poked his head out the door and saw a line of poor and homeless types following the food carriers.

"Hey, guys!" he shouted to his family. "We've got company . . . and how!"

"Come right on in," Mom said, greeting the folks at the door. Many of them wore torn and dirty clothing. Some smelled like they hadn't taken a shower in a week. Others looked like it had been that long since they'd had a decent meal. But none of this stopped Mom. In fact, it gave her all the more reasons to smile and direct the people toward the makeshift buffet on the counter.

While she did so, Nick and Dad busily collected chairs, stools, even upside-down buckets—anything for their guests to sit on. Just then, a familiar face pushed through the crowd toward Grandma. "Mrs. Martin?" It was Julia, the mail carrier, and with her was her roommate!

Meanwhile, Dad had turned and found himself face-to-face with Crazy Jim—the man he had given a quarter to just the day before.

"Splendid party, old boy," Crazy Jim said. He reached into his pocket and handed Dad a quarter. "Here's a little something to help with the expenses." he grinned. "I presume you can break a quarter?"

Suddenly Dad remembered why the man looked so familiar, and his face turned beet red as he recalled his stinginess the day before. With a chuckle, Crazy Jim flipped the quarter into the air. Dad caught it and, to help lighten the moment, he managed to find a dime to give back. Now both men laughed.

It would be a long time before Dad forgot the little lesson he learned that day.

Come to think of it, it would be a long time before anyone in the family forgot what they learned.

NINE
Wrapping Up

A few minutes later Nick returned from his room upstairs. In his hand was the model glider that had been hanging above his bed.

"Ilie," he shouted as he threaded his way through the crowd of people. "I want you to have this."

The Romanian boy's eyes widened. "Oh, Nick," he said, backing away, "I cannot accept thees."

"Please," Nick insisted, pushing the glider into Ilie's hands, "I want you to have it. It's just my way of . . . what I mean is, I'm sorry for . . . "

"Eet ees OK, Nick," Ilie smiled. "If you had come to visit me during World Cup, I would have thought you were 'Dweeb-O-Matic,' too."

Nick broke into a grin and gave the smaller boy a quick hug.

Michael looked across the room and saw the two boys hugging. "Ahh, Meesus Martin," he chortled, "I see your son has learned well our way of greeting, yes?"

"We've all learned a lot from you," Mom said as she set a stack of dishes in the sink. "I want to thank you for reminding us what Thanksgiving is really about."

"You're welcome!" Michael said with his big laugh. "Een Romania, I think we should start such a holiday . . . 'Day to be thankful!' Every day we should be thankful, no?"

Mom nodded.

He went on jokingly, "I do not know where we will get the Indians and the Pilgrims, though, but this," he said, pointing to the cabbage casserole, "ees a good start. A greater American dish I never have had!"

After a moment of stunned silence, Mom broke into delighted laughter.

Several hours later, Jamie carefully made her way down the stairs. Who knows how many times she'd buzzed her intercom before finally giving up. At last she appeared on the kitchen stairway wearing her robe, sunglasses (measles don't like bright lights), and gobs of white goop to help stop the itching.

By now most of the guests were gone. But not the pans and plates piled high in the sink.

"Man," she muttered, "I get sick for a few days and look what happens! My family opens a restaurant." She tilted down her sunglasses for a better look. "I better get well . . . fast!"

Suddenly Steven appeared. It's hard to guess who was the more surprised: Jamie, seeing a strange kid in worn-out clothing standing in the middle of her kitchen, or Steven, seeing the white-gooped monster-face dressed in sunglasses and a robe.

Jamie was the first to speak. "Who are you?" she demanded. Then she scowled. "You look awful."

"So what's *your* excuse?" Steven shot back. "Premature acne?"

He stepped up for a closer look.

"Stay back!" she ordered. "Can't you tell, I've got the measles! She took off her sunglasses and explained, "These are for protecting my eyes, and this stuff," she pointed to the goop on her face, "is to keep the bumps from itching so much."

"Measles," Steven shrugged. "I already had them . . . last spring. No problem. The chicken pox, though, that was bad news! I was one gigantic bag of itch."

Not to be outdone it was Jamie's turn to brag. "Chicken pox?! Kid's stuff. I had strep throat last winter and you wouldn't believe the—"

She was interrupted by a couple of tattered street people heading toward the back door.

"What's going on?" she demanded. "Am I in an old 'Twilight Zone' rerun?"

"Your mom and dad invited us, you know, from the Back Alley Mission."

"You mean you're . . . homeless people?" Jamie asked, looking at him like he was from Jupiter.

"Don't call me that!" he said threateningly. "I got a family, and we got a home!" He paused for a minute, a little ashamed of his outburst. He shrugged and continued, "Though it ain't much of a home."

Then he brightened. "But it won't be that way for long."

"How come?" Jamie asked.

"Because your dad and mom promised to help my dad find work." He suddenly broke out laughing. "Your mom was so funny!"

"Mom? Funny?" Jamie asked skeptically. Moms are for feeding you, making you clean up your room, and checking over your homework—not for being funny.

"Yeah!" Steven grinned. "She turned all red when she found out we were living in refrigerator boxes. I thought she was gonna slug somebody. Then she grabbed my mom and yanked her outta the room, jabbering about some nice old Indian down the street—a Mr. Ravenhill who has a whole house to himself."

"Steven!" a voice suddenly called from the back door.

Jamie turned to look as a woman entered. She must have been Steven's mom, 'cause it looked like they shopped at the same store: "Threads 'R' Us."

"It's all set, sweetheart," his mother said. "Mr. Ravenhill is more than willing for us to stay with him. We'd better get going, though, before it gets dark."

"Great!" Steven called. Then turning back to Jamie he shrugged. "Guess we'll see you around."

"Yeah . . . sure."

Jamie watched as the kid headed out the door to join his family. He seemed a nice enough guy. And if he was going to stay at Mr. Ravenhill's place for a while, they'd be like neighbors. Maybe they'd even become friends. Who knew.

Jamie sighed, gave a little scratch around her collar and headed back up the steps.

As Jamie girl headed up the stairs, I figured it was time for me to do a little "heading up" of my own. But not by mere mortal foot power, no-siree-bob. Instead, it would be my magnificent McGee Mind Power . . .

I stood on the middle of the dining room table and blew into a giant hose attached to an even gianter blimp. Not that I'm full of hot air, mind you, but with this spy business on the downturn, I was looking into new career opportunities. Anything to allow me to use all my fancy-schmanzy surveillance cameras and stuff.

And what could be smarter than making a fortune with my special "McGee-Cam."

I finished inflating the blimp, pulled out the hose, and shoved a giant cork into the hole.

Now I was ready.

Step aside Goodyear—it was time for the new and improved . . . McGee-Year blimp. I would be the one videotaping all the bowl games; I would be the one covering all the parades; I would be the one squeezing his magnificently pudgy body into that magnificently small passenger cabin . . .

Aaagh, Ugggh, Romf . . . Ahhhh . . .

Home, sweet matchbox. I don't want to say the passenger compartment was small, but it was the first time I could scratch my foot by blinking my eyelids.

I pulled anchor and the blimp began to rise. Faster and faster. Higher and higher. Soon we were millions of miles above the dining room table.

OK, make that thousands of feet.

All right, all right. But eighteen inches is better than nothing.

The point is, I could see everything . . . well, at least the important things, like every ounce of left-over food. Carefully, I maneuvered the blimp's controls. Talk about complicated. It was worse than Dad's new TV remote. I had no idea what I was doing. But since when has that ever stopped me, the great McGee?

And then I saw it. Ah yes, the remains of our turkey. Actually, it was a bird's-eye view of the turkey. (Get it? Turkey? Bird's-eye? I suppose you think you could do better?)

Unfortunately, I was so impressed by my incredible wit (it takes so little to impress me!) that I didn't notice the way the little cork in the blimp had started to work its way out of the not-so-little hole.

Quicker than you can ask, "How many times have I seen this in Saturday morning cartoons?" the cork popped out and I began zipping around the room.

"Yeeooooooow!" I cried, hanging on for dear life.

Any fool knew I had to pull up on the controls to keep the blimp's nose pointed toward the sky. So I did what any fool would do. I grabbed the controls and pushed them straight down. (Some people can't tell their lefts from their rights. Well, I can't tell my ups from my downs.) Soon I had that blimp in the world's steepest nosedive.

"Mayday! Mayday!" I cried. "I'm goin' in! I'm goin' in!"

I couldn't have been more right . . .

SPLAT!

I did "go in." Right into the bowl of gravy.

A moment later I surfaced, covered in the thick brown goo. But every cloud has a silver lining. This stuff was . . .

SLURP . . .

. . . pretty tasty.

GLUG, GLUG, GLUG . . .

With any luck I'd have it all drunk by . . .

CHUG, CHUG, CHUG . . .

. . . my next exciting little adventure.

Stay tuned, food fanatics. Who knows what tasty treat of an adventure lies ahead? Who knows what this king of the junk food junkies will eat next? Freeze-dried asparagus with chocolate sauce? Dill pickles covered in Dijon mustard? The mind staggers with possibilities. The stomach retches with nausea.

But first things first. Now it's just me and this bowl of gravy. Hey, it's like I always say, "Into every bowl of gravy, a little turkey must fall."

Ho-ho, ha-ha, hee-hee . . .

BURP!!

See ya around!